Nari
the Ninja Pet Sitter

Shawna Yant

Printed in the United States of America

First Printing, 2019

ISBN 978-1-074975-17-3 Paperback
ISBN 978-0-578-53192-2 Hardcover

I dedicate this book to the dreamers, doers, and thinkers. To the people that are not afraid to pursue their passions and initiatives that make them happy because life is too short to live any other way.

Hi there! I'm Nari the Ninja! If you're looking for tips on how to be an awesome pet sitter, you've come to the right place!

There are so many wonderful reasons to pet sit! You get to meet all sorts of animals and make new friends. But pet sitting isn't always easy-peasy. That's why I made this guide to teach you the important skills you'll need to be a ninja pet sitter like me!.

Part 1: How to Catch a Cat

Cats are sneaky creatures that can hide in the weirdest of places! Sometimes when they are hiding, they *really* don't want to be found. When pet sitting cats, it's important to know how to coax them out of their hiding places.

Take Chloe, for instance. She loved her mom and didn't hide from her because they were close, but when Chloe saw me, she darted off as quick as lightning! Chloe had a condition, and it made it difficult for her to breathe, so she had to have medicine whenever she was sneezing a lot or wheezing.

When Chloe first ran off, I wasn't worried, but then I started to hear faint sneezing noises! I realized that Chloe was going to need her medicine, but I could only hear her and not see her. I looked under the couches, the beds and in the closets. I could not find her.

I noticed a box of treats and decided to use them as bait to get Chloe to come out of her hiding place.

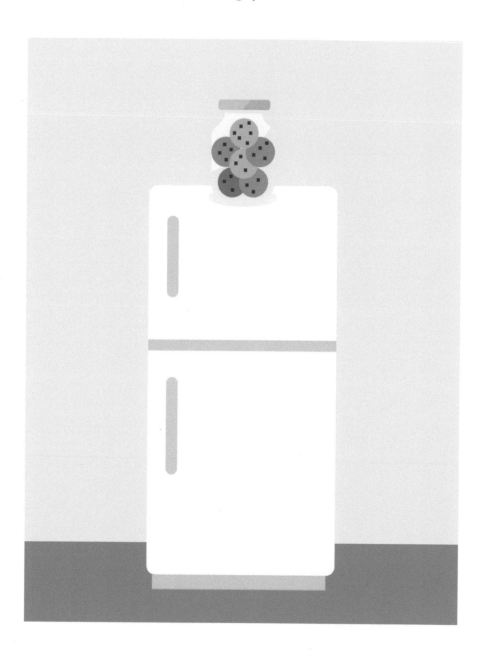

Next , I grabbed Chloe's medicine. I shook the bag of treats and called Chloe's name softly. After I placed a few treats on the ground, it didn't take long for her to come out.

While she was eating them, I quickly scooped her up and gave her the medicine.

Ninja Tip: Never pull a cat out from their hiding place, especially if they are under a bed. Removing a cat from their hiding place can cause unnecessary stress and anxiety for the pet.

Part 2: How to Walk a Dog

Walking a dog may seem like an easy task, but there are lots of things you should be mindful of because dogs love to chase things. If you're not careful, the dog you are walking may try to bolt after a squirrel and run right into the street!

When I was walking a dog named Dudley, a stray dog came towards us! Dudley was much smaller than him, so I carefully crossed the street away from the stray dog. I thought we were in the clear, but the stray dog crossed the street too!

With the dog quickly approaching, I decided the best way to protect Dudley was to stand my ground. I shielded Dudley and stood up as straight as I could. I started yelling and waving my arms in crazy directions. The stray dog stopped coming towards us and turned away. With the stray dog gone, Dudley and I were able to safely continue our walk.

Ninja Tip: Humans can't outrun loose dogs, so you have to use your brain to outsmart them!

Part 3: How to Care for a Lizard

I was asked to watch a lizard named Lenny. I had never watched a lizard before, but I was excited about this new experience! Lenny was a bearded dragon, and he lived in a terrarium. A terrarium is like a glass rectangle home for lizards. There were rocks and tree pieces for him to climb on and sand that he could bury himself in.

After some studying, I knew his tank needed to be an exact temperature. That he needed to eat live bugs regularly. I didn't know why his skin started falling off! It was falling off in big pieces, and thought Lenny must be sick!

I called Lisa, Lenny's owner, and explained what was happening. She told me that Lenny was molting and that it was normal! Lizards shed their skin when they grow!

Ninja Tip: Did you know bearded dragons can't eat avocados or fireflies? Don't let your lizard eat these; it could be deadly!

I hope you enjoyed these tips! Each day is a new adventure filled with exciting experiences. If you like exploring the outdoors, dogs make great companions. Cats have minds of their own, and when they bond with their owners, they share a special relationship. Not everyone has dogs and cats. Some people have rabbits, hamsters, birds, and horses too! Every pet is special and unique, so take the time to see what this world has to offer, and you might find your perfect match!